Muggie Maggie

A couple of days later, Maggie's mother said, "The school psychologist wrote us a letter."

Maggie's feelings were hurt. He had seemed like such a nice man. She had learned to be suspicious of letters from school. This was not the first.

Her mother continued. "He says it will be interesting to see how long it will take you to decide to write cursive."

"Oh," said Maggie.

"How long do you think that will be?" asked her mother.

"Maybe forever," said Maggie, beginning to wish she had never started the whole thing.

Enjoy all of
Beverly Cleary's books

FEATURING RAMONA QUIMBY:

Beezus and Ramona

Ramona the Pest

Ramona the Brave

Ramona and Her Father

Ramona and Her Mother

Ramona Quimby, Age 8

Ramona Forever

Ramona's World

FEATURING HENRY HUGGINS:

Henry Huggins

Henry and Beezus

Henry and Ribsy

Henry and the Paper Route

Henry and the Clubhouse

Ribsy

FEATURING RALPH MOUSE:

The Mouse and the Motorcycle

Runaway Ralph

Ralph S. Mouse

MORE GREAT FICTION BY BEVERLY CLEARY:

Ellen Tebbits

Otis Spofford

Fifteen

The Luckiest Girl

Jean and Johnny

Emily's Runaway Imagination

Sister of the Bride

Mitch and Amy

Socks

Dear Mr. Henshaw

Muggie Maggie

Strider

Two Times the Fun

AND DON'T MISS BEVERLY CLEARY'S AUTOBIOGRAPHIES:

A Girl from Yamhill

My Own Two Feet

Beverly Cleary

Muggie Maggie

ILLUSTRATED BY
Tracy Dockray

HarperTrophy®
An Imprint of HarperCollinsPublishers

Muggie Maggie
Copyright © 1990 by Beverly Cleary
All rights reserved. Printed in the United States of
America. No part of this book may be
used or reproduced in any manner whatsoever without
written permission except in the case of brief quotations
embodied in critical articles and reviews.
For information address HarperCollins Children's Books,
a division of HarperCollins Publishers,
10 East 53rd Street, New York, NY 10022.
www.harpercollinschildrens.com

Library of Congress Catalog Card Number: 89-38959
ISBN 978-0-380-71087-4
❖
Reillustrated Harper Trophy edition, 2008

11 12 13 LP/CW 60 59 58 57 56 55 54 53 52 51

To a third-grade girl who wondered why
no one ever wrote a book to help
third graders read cursive writing

Chapter 1

After her first day in the third grade, Maggie Schultz jumped off the school bus when it stopped at her corner. "Bye, Jo Ann," she called to the girl who was her best friend, sometimes. "See you tomorrow." Maggie was happy to escape from sixth-grade boys who called her a cootie and from fourth-grade boys who insisted the third grade was awful, cursive writing hard, and Mrs. Leeper, the teacher, mean.

Her dog, Kisser, was waiting for her. When Maggie knelt to hug him, Kisser licked her face. He was a young, eager dog the Schultzes had chosen from the S.P.C.A.'s Pick-a-Pet page in the newspaper. "A friendly cockapoo looking for a child to love" was the description under his picture, a description that proved to be right.

"Come on, Kisser." Maggie ran home with her fair hair flying and her dog springing along beside her.

When Maggie and Kisser burst through the kitchen door, her mother said, "Hi there, Angelface. How did things go today?" She held Kisser away from the refrigerator with her foot while she put away milk cartons and vegetables. Mrs. Schultz was good at standing on one foot because five mornings a week she taught exercise classes to overweight women.

"Mrs. Leeper is nice, sort of," began

Maggie, "except she didn't make me a monitor and she put Jo Ann at a different table."

"Too bad," said Mrs. Schultz.

Maggie continued. "Courtney sits on one side of me and Kelly on the other and that Kirby Jones, who sits across from me, kept pushing the table into my stomach."

"And what did you do?" Mrs. Schultz was taking eggs out of a carton and setting them in the white plastic egg tray in the refrigerator.

"Pushed it back." Maggie thought a moment before she said, "Mrs. Leeper said we are going to have a happy third grade."

"That's nice." Mrs. Schultz smiled as she closed the refrigerator, but Maggie was doubtful about a teacher who forecast happiness. How did she know? Still, Maggie wanted her teacher to be happy.

"Kisser needs exercise," Mrs. Schultz said. "Why don't you take him outside and give him a workout?" Maggie's mother thought everyone, dogs included, needed exercise.

Maggie enjoyed chasing Kisser around the backyard, ducking, dodging, and throwing a dirty tennis ball, wet with dog spit, for him until he collapsed, panting, and she was out of breath from running and laughing.

Refreshed and much more cheerful, Maggie was flipping through television channels with the remote control, trying to find funny commercials, when her father came home from work. "Daddy! Daddy!" she cried, running to meet him. He picked her up, kissed her, and asked, "How's my Goldilocks?" When he set her down, he kissed his wife.

"Tired?" Mrs. Schultz asked.

"Traffic gets worse every day," he answered.

"Was it your turn to make the coffee?" demanded Maggie.

"That's right," grumped Mr. Schultz, half-pretending.

Other than talking with people who came to see him, Maggie did not really understand what her father did in his office. She did know he made coffee every other day because Ms. Madden, his secretary, said she did not go to work in an office to make coffee. He should take his turn. Ms. Madden was such an excellent secretary—one who could spell, punctuate, and type—that Mr. Schultz put up with his share of coffee-making. Maggie found this so funny that she always asked about the coffee.

"Did Ms. Madden send me a present?" Maggie asked. Her father's secretary often sent Maggie a little present: a tiny bottle of shampoo from a hotel, a free sample of perfume, and once, an eraser shaped like a duck. Maggie felt grown-up when she wrote thank-you notes on their home computer.

"Not today." Mr. Schultz tousled Maggie's hair and went to change into his jogging clothes.

When dinner was on the table and the family, exercised, happy, and hungry, was seated, Maggie chose the right moment to break her big news. "We start cursive this week," she said with a gusty sigh that was supposed to impress her parents with the hard work that lay ahead.

Instead, they laughed. Maggie was annoyed. Cursive was *serious*. She tossed her hair, which was perfect for tossing, waving, and curling to her shoulders, the sort of hair that made women say, "What wouldn't you give for hair like that?" or, in sad voices, "I used to have hair that color."

"Don't look so gloomy," said Maggie's father. "You'll survive."

How did he know? Maggie scowled, still hurting from being laughed at, and said,

"Cursive is dumb. It's all wrinkled and stuck together, and I can't see why I am supposed to do it." This was a new thought that popped into her mind that moment.

"Because everyone writes cursive," said Mrs. Schultz. "Or almost everybody."

"But I can write print, or I can use the computer," said Maggie, arguing mostly just to be arguing.

"I'm sure you'll enjoy cursive once you start," said Mrs. Schultz in that brisk, positive way that always made Maggie feel contrary.

I will not enjoy it, thought Maggie, and she said, "All those loops and squiggles. I don't think I'll do it."

"Of course you will," said her father. "That's why you go to school."

This made Maggie even more contrary. "I'm not going to write cursive, and nobody can make me. So there."

"Ho-ho," said her mother so cheerfully

that Maggie felt three times as contrary.

Mr. Schultz's smile flattened into a straight line. "Just get busy, do what your teacher says, and learn it."

The way her father spoke pushed Maggie further into contrariness. She stabbed her fork into her baked potato so the handle stood up straight, then she broke off a piece of her beef patty with her fingers and fed it to Kisser.

"Maggie, *please*," said her mother. "Your father has had a hard day, and I haven't had such a great day myself." After teaching her exercise classes in the morning, Mrs. Schultz spent her afternoons running errands for her family: dry cleaner, bank, gas station, market, post office.

Maggie pulled her fork out of her baked potato. Kisser licked his chops and looked up at her with hope in his brown eyes, his tail wagging. "Kisser is lucky," she said. "He doesn't have to learn cursive." When her dog heard his name, he stood up and placed his front paws on her lap.

"Now you're being silly, Maggie," said her father. "Down, Kisser, you old nuisance."

Maggie was indignant. "Kisser is not a nuisance. Kisser is a loving dog," she informed her father.

"Don't try to change the subject." Mr. Schultz, irritated with Maggie, smiled at his wife, who was pouring him a cup of coffee.

"Books are not written in cursive," Maggie pointed out. "I can read chapter books, and not everyone in my class is good at that."

Mr. Schultz sipped his coffee. "True," he admitted, "but many things are written in cursive. Memos, many letters, grocery lists, checks, lots of things."

"I can write letters in printing, and I never write those other things," argued

Maggie, "so *I am not going to learn cursive.*"
She tossed her hair and asked to be excused.

Kisser felt that he, too, was excused. He
trotted after Maggie and jumped up on her
bed. As she hugged him, Maggie overheard
her mother say, "I don't know what gets into
Maggie. Most of the time she behaves herself, and then suddenly she doesn't."

"Contrary kid," said her father.

Chapter 2

The next day, after the third-grade monitors had led the flag salute, changed the date on the calendar, fed the hamster, and done all the housekeeping chores that third-grade monitors do in the morning, Mrs. Leeper faced her class and said, "Today is going to be a happy day."

The third grade looked hopeful.

"Today we take a big step in growing up," said Mrs. Leeper. "We are going to learn cursive handwriting. We are going to learn to make our letters flow together." Mrs. Leeper made *flow* sound like a long, long word as she waved her hand in a graceful flowing motion.

She calls that exciting, thought Maggie, slumping in her chair.

"How many of you have ridden on a roller coaster?" asked Mrs. Leeper. Half the members of the class raised their hands. Mrs. Leeper wrote on the chalkboard:

a   c   d   m   n

"Many letters start up slowly, just like a roller coaster, and then drop down," she said, and she traced over the first stroke of each letter with colored chalk. Then she went on to demonstrate how the roller coaster climbed almost straight up:

b f l t

After the paper monitor passed out paper, the class practiced, not whole letters but roller-coaster strokes:

ᴄ ᴄ ᴄ   ⌿⌿⌿

Maggie did as she was told until she grew bored and began to draw one long roller-coaster line that rose and fell, turned and twisted, and rose again. So many of the class needed help with their strokes that Mrs. Leeper did not get around to Maggie.

The next day, after strokes, the class practiced whole letters, some with loops that went up, some with loops that went down. This was difficult. The third grade frowned, worried, struggled, and asked Mrs. Leeper whether they were doing it right. Then they learned to connect letters with straight lines.

Maggie went on drawing roller coasters until Mrs. Leeper noticed.

"Why, Maggie," she said, "why haven't you been working on your loops and lines?"

"I am working," said Maggie, "on roller coasters."

Mrs. Leeper looked thoughtfully at Maggie, who tried to look happy. "Roller coasters are not cursive," said the teacher.

"I know," agreed Maggie, "but I don't need cursive. I use our computer."

"Maggie, I think you had better stay after school so we can have a little talk," said Mrs. Leeper.

"I have to catch my bus," said Maggie with her sweetest smile.

That afternoon, Maggie examined cursive writing wherever she found it. "Why

does your writing on the grocery list lean over backward?" she asked her mother. "Mrs. Leeper says letters should lean forward as if they were walking against the wind."

"I'm left-handed, and my teachers didn't show me how to turn my paper," answered Mrs. Schultz.

"And what are those little circles floating around?" asked Maggie.

Her mother laughed. "When I was in junior high, girls often made circles instead of dots over their *i*'s. We thought it was artistic or something. I don't really remember."

That evening, Maggie stood at her father's side as he wrote a letter on the computer. When he pulled the paper out of the printer, he picked up a pen and wrote at the bottom:

Sydney Schultz

"What does that say?" asked Maggie.

"That's how I sign my name," said her father. "Sydney Schultz."

"You didn't close your loops," Maggie pointed out. "You are supposed to close loops on letters that have pieces that hang down." She had learned a thing or two in spite of herself.

"Oops," said Mr. Schultz, and he closed his loops.

ChapTer 3

Maggie began to enjoy cursive time. She experimented with letters leaning over backward and decorated with little circles, the way her mother dotted her *i*'s. She wrote messy *g*'s with long straight tails, the way her father made his *y*'s.

"Why, Maggie," said Mrs. Leeper. "I find your cursive very untidy."

"I'm writing like a grown-up," Maggie explained.

The result was Mrs. Leeper's asking Maggie's mother to come to school for a conference. That day, Mrs. Schultz had to fill the gas tank of the car, go to the bank, buy paper for the computer, and take Kisser to the veterinarian for his shot—all this after teaching exercise classes in the morning. She was not smiling when she reached school, still wearing her warm-up suit. She handed Kisser's leash to Maggie so she could take care of him during her conference with Mrs. Leeper.

Kisser was so happy to see a playground full of children that he wanted to jump up on everyone. Maggie had to hold on to his leash with both hands when her friends gathered around to ask why Mrs. Schultz was talking to the teacher.

Jo Ann answered for Maggie. "Maybe Mrs. Leeper wants her to be room mother or something."

"I bet," said Kirby on his way to the bus.

"What did she say?" demanded Maggie when her mother returned and everyone had boarded buses. "What did Mrs. Leeper say about me?"

"Down, Kisser!" Mrs. Schultz sounded cross. "Mrs. Leeper said you are a reluctant cursive writer who has not reached cursive-writing readiness, and perhaps you are too immature to write it."

Maggie was indignant. "I am not!" she said. "I am Gifted and Talented." Some people were Gifted and Talented, and some people weren't. At least, that was what teachers thought. Maybe no one had told Mrs. Leeper how Gifted and Talented she was. Maggie's mother drove home without saying one single word. Maggie hugged Kisser, who was so grateful that he licked her face, which she found comforting. Someone loved her.

For several days, just for fun, Maggie drew fancy letters at cursive time, and then Mrs. Leeper told her that Mr. Galloway, the principal, wanted to see her in his office. On her way, Maggie, filled with dread, dawdled as long as she felt she could get away with it.

"Hello there, Maggie," said Mr. Galloway. "Sit down and let's have a little talk."

Maggie sat. She never enjoyed what grown-ups called "a little talk."

Mr. Galloway smiled, leaned back in his chair, and placed his fingertips together like an *A*, with his thumbs for the crossbar. A printed *A*, of course. "Maggie, Mrs. Leeper tells me you are not writing cursive. Can you tell me why?"

Maggie swung her legs, stared at a picture of George Washington on the wall, nibbled a hangnail. Mr. Galloway waited. Finally, Maggie had to say something. "I don't want to."

"I see." Mr. Galloway spoke as if Maggie had said something very important that required serious thought, lots of it.

"And why don't you want to?" asked the principal after a long silence, during which Maggie studied the way he combed his hair over his bald spot.

"I just don't want to," said Maggie. "I use a computer."

Mr. Galloway nodded as if he understood. "That's all, Maggie," he said. "Thank you for coming in."

That evening, Mrs. Leeper telephoned Maggie's mother to say that the principal had reported Maggie was not motivated to write cursive. "That means you don't want to," Mrs. Schultz explained to Maggie.

"That's what I told him," said Maggie, who couldn't see what all the fuss was about.

"Maggie!" cried her mother. "What are

we going to do with you?"

"I'll motivate you, young lady," said Mr. Schultz. "No more computer for you. You stay strictly away from it."

Mrs. Schultz had more to say. "Tomorrow, Maggie is to see the school psychologist." She looked worried, Mr. Schultz looked grim, and Maggie was frightened. A psychologist sounded scary. Kisser understood. He licked Maggie's hand to make her feel better.

As it turned out, Maggie loved the psychologist, who talked in a quiet voice and let her play with some toys while he asked gentle questions about her family, her dog, her teachers—nothing important. He asked about her times tables, and almost as an afterthought, he inquired, "How do you like cursive writing?"

"Okay," answered Maggie, because he was a grown-up.

A couple of days later, Maggie's mother said, "The school psychologist wrote us a letter."

Maggie's feelings were hurt. He had seemed like such a nice man. She had learned to be suspicious of letters from school. This was not the first.

Mrs. Schultz continued. "He says it will be interesting to see how long it will take you to decide to write cursive."

"Oh," said Maggie.

"How long do you think that will be?" asked Mrs. Schultz.

"Maybe forever," said Maggie, beginning to wish she had never started the whole thing.

ChapTer 4

Maggie had grown bored with not writing cursive, but by now the whole third grade was interested in her revolt. Each day, they watched to see whether she gave in. Her friends talked about it at lunchtime. In the hall, she overheard a fourth grader say, "There goes that girl who won't write cursive." Many people thought she was brave; others thought she was acting stupid. Obviously, Maggie could not back down now. She had to protect her pride.

Courtney and Kelly, best friends who sat opposite one another, did not approve of Maggie.

Courtney said, "Only first and second graders print."

Kelly said, "I think you are acting dumb, Maggie."

Jo Ann whispered from the next table. "If you are having trouble, maybe I can help you on Saturday."

"I'm *not* having trouble," Maggie whispered back. "I just don't want to do it." Then she worried. What if others thought Gifted and Talented Maggie couldn't write cursive if she wanted to?

Mrs. Leeper handed out individual papers with each person's name, first and last, written in perfect cursive at the top. "Today we practice our signatures," she said, and she looked at Maggie. "Even if we write letters on computers, we must sign them in our own handwriting."

Maggie studied her neatly written name. If she wrote "Maggie Schultz" and not one letter more, would this be giving in? Not really, she decided, not if she wrote like a grown-up.

While Kirby—a boy who always did what he was told, more or less—gripped his pencil, pressing down so hard he broke the point and had to go to the pencil sharpener, and Courtney and Kelly wrote with pencils whispering daintily across their papers, Maggie wrote her name the way her father wrote his:

Maggie Schultz

On the next line, she wrote with her left

hand, which was difficult:

Maggie Schultz

Kirby worked so hard that he needed a rest. He pushed the table into Maggie's stomach. Maggie pushed it back.

"Mrs. Leeper!" said Courtney. "Kirby and Maggie are wrecking our cursive."

"They do it all the time," said Kelly.

This brought Mrs. Leeper to their table. "See, Mrs. Leeper," said Courtney, pointing. "That is where Kirby pushed the table."

"And this is where Maggie pushed it back," said Kelly.

"I'm sure they won't do it again." Mrs. Leeper tried to look happy as she paused beside Maggie.

Maggie quickly curved her arm around her paper and bowed her head as if she was working very, very hard.

Mrs. Leeper, who often told the class she had eyes in the back of her head, had already seen Maggie's work, if one could really call it work. "Maggie, why are you writing with your left hand when you are right-handed?" she wanted to know.

"That's the way my mother writes," explained Maggie.

Mrs. Leeper removed the pencil from Maggie's left hand and placed it in her right. "And where are the loops on your *g*'s that we talked about? Your *l* and *t* are leaning over backward. We don't want our telephone poles to tip over, do we?"

"I guess not," said Maggie.

"Take your paper home and do it over," said Mrs. Leeper, "and we must close our *a*. Your name is not Muggie."

Maggie knew she was done for.

"Muggie Maggie," whispered Kirby, as Maggie had expected.

"You keep quiet." Maggie pushed the table into his stomach.

"Mrs. Leeper!" cried Courtney and Kelly at the same time.

"I thought we were going to have a happy teacher today," said Mrs. Leeper. "Let's be good citizens."

Maggie was sure she would not have a happy recess, and she did not. Everyone shouted "Muggie Maggie! Muggie Maggie!" Kirby started it, of course. He was not a good citizen.

ChapTer 5

Later that week, Mr. Schultz brought Maggie a present from Ms. Madden, a ball-point pen that wrote in either red or blue ink.

"Just what I've always wanted." Maggie was filled with love for Ms. Madden, the one grown-up who, Maggie felt, did not pick on her.

"Can I thank her on the computer?"

asked Maggie, testing her father.

"You may not. The computer is off limits." Mr. Schultz was annoyingly cheerful. "Use your new pen."

Maggie was not surprised. Her father always meant what he said. She went to her room and, with Kisser resting his nose on her foot, went to work. Her printing was not as neat as it once had been because she was out of practice. She wrote one letter in blue, the next in red, over and over:

Dear Ms. Madden,
Thank you for the pen. I like it.
              Love,
                Maggie

After a moment's thought, she added:

Sorry So Sloggy

There. Maggie, pleased with her work, folded the letter, sealed it in an envelope, printed Ms. Madden on the front, and slipped it into her father's briefcase, with the virtuous feeling of having done what was expected of her.

The next evening, Mr. Schultz brought home an envelope for Maggie, who tore it open. The note, as she had expected, was from Ms. Madden and was neatly typed, except for one consonant. It read:

Dear Maggie,
If you are really

S orry
o
loggy

(or did you mean sloppy?)
Why didn't you copy
your letter over?
Love,

Hilda Madden

Maggie's eyes filled with tears, she felt so ashamed. Now even Ms. Madden, along with everyone else, was picking on her.

Mrs. Schultz, seeing Maggie's tears, asked to read the note. Then she said gently, "Well Angelface, why didn't you do your letter over?"

Maggie sniffed. "I thought Ms. Madden would understand."

Maggie's father took his turn at reading the embarrassing note. "Of course Ms. Madden wouldn't understand," he said. "Ms. Madden is a secretary who is always neat and accurate."

"Well, I don't want to be a secretary," said Maggie, thinking of several neat, accurate girls in the third grade. "I'm going to be an astronaut or a meter maid."

"Good for you, Goldilocks," said her father, and he rumpled her hair.

CHaPTeR 6

One morning, Maggie noticed Mrs. Leeper whispering with other teachers in the hall. They glanced at Maggie, who scrunched down, trying to look invisible so they wouldn't talk about her.

When class started, Mrs. Leeper said, "Boys and girls, let's have a happy teacher today." She said that so often, no one paid any attention. Then she pointed to words she had written on the chalkboard:

mouth of September
mice day

The words made the class laugh, but Maggie did not see anything funny. Mrs. Leeper said, "Maggie, can you tell us what is wrong with these words?"

That was the moment when Maggie discovered she could not read cursive. She shook her head while others, eager to point out errors, waved their hands.

Later in the day, Mrs. Leeper announced, "Class, we need a message monitor. Who wants to be our message monitor?"

Even though she did not expect to be chosen because she was not a person who made Mrs. Leeper happy, Maggie raised her hand. So did the rest of the class, except Kirby, who never wanted to be a monitor for anything and who, at the moment, was under the table.

"Maggie, you may be our message monitor," said Mrs. Leeper.

"She means Muggie," whispered Kirby, coming up from under the table, where he had been figuring out how the legs were fastened to the top.

"Me?" said Maggie.

"Yes, you," said Mrs. Leeper with a happy smile. "And here is a note for you to take to Mr. Galloway." She handed Maggie an envelope. "Please wait for an answer."

Maggie lost no time in escaping to the freedom of the hall, where no one supervised her. The envelope was not sealed. Peeking was cheating, Maggie told herself. Bravely and honestly, Maggie carried the note halfway to the principal's office. Then she stopped and thought, One peek won't hurt, not if it's quick. If the envelope was not sealed, it must be all right to look inside.

She might have guessed—cursive writing. Maggie could not figure out the note, which read:

When is this girl ever going to decide to write cursive?

Maggie recognized the question mark and decided Mrs. Leeper was probably asking for more work sheets or something equally boring.

"Hello there, Maggie," said the principal when she held out the note. While Maggie waited, Mr. Galloway wrote a short answer, which he put in the same envelope. He crossed out his name and wrote Mrs. Leeper's name in its place. The school could not afford to waste envelopes.

"Take this to your teacher," he said with a big smile. "And thank you, Maggie."

I won't look, I won't look, Maggie told

herself. What would be the use when the note was written in cursive? Maggie walked more and more slowly. Was it wrong to look at something she could not read? Of course not, Maggie decided, and she slipped the note out of the envelope.

Mr. Galloway's cursive was not as neat as Mrs. Leeper's, which did not seem right to Maggie. A principal's writing should be better than a teacher's.

Maggie will decide to read and write cursive sooner or later. It looks like later.

Maggie studied Mr. Galloway's loops and curves until one word jumped out at her: *Maggie.* She was shocked. What was Mr. Galloway saying about her? Maggie felt her cheeks turn red. Quickly, she replaced the note and hurried to her classroom as if she was carrying something hot. Mrs. Leeper gave her a sharp look and said, "Thank you, Maggie," before she read what the principal had written. Then she smiled, once more a happy teacher.

Suddenly, Maggie found cursive interesting. How could she read people's letters if she could not read cursive? She couldn't. Maggie, Gifted and Talented Maggie, felt defeat.

ChapTer 7

For the next few days Maggie was a busy message monitor because Mrs. Leeper sent her hurrying to one room after another. She was even sent to the library. The envelope grew shabby. Most messages contained her name; others did not. Maggie snatched moments in the hall to try to figure out words, but all she learned was that some teachers were careless about joining letters without lifting pencil from paper.

"How come you're delivering so many messages?" asked Kirby.

"Because she can't read cursive," said Courtney.

"And Mrs. Leeper knows she can't snoop," said Kelly.

"Mrs. Leeper wants me to deliver them," said Maggie. "It makes her happy."

"I bet," said Kirby.

On her way to the first-grade room, Maggie discovered that all of Mrs. Leeper's notes looked exactly alike, which was funny peculiar, not funny ha-ha. Feeling big and important in front of first graders, Maggie wondered about this as she listened to the little children play with the Velcro fasteners on their shoes. *Rip-rip-rip.* This teacher's answer to Mrs. Leeper did not contain her name, so Maggie was not much interested. It read:

Keep it up. You will wear this kid down yet.

In the sixth-grade room, Maggie felt as if she had shrunk because all the sixth graders stared at her while the teacher, a tall man with a ferocious beard, read the note.

"There's the cootie," she heard a boy whisper.

Maggie tossed her hair. The class tittered. Maggie wondered whether the boys called their teacher's beard a cootie motel.

The man glanced at Maggie, grinned, and wrote a note on the back of an old spelling test. Then he crossed out his name on the ragged envelope, replaced it with Mrs. Leeper's name in one of the few spaces left, and handed it to Maggie, who was grateful to escape to the hall.

When she peeked, Maggie found her

own name, just as she had in other notes, but this time she found it twice. The note read:

I once had a bright kid like Maggie who thought she couldn't read cursive She really could when she tried, but she wouldn't. Sounds like Maggie.

Maggie, desperate to read, discovered this teacher was careless about joining letters. If she had time, maybe she could puzzle them out, but she knew that she was expected back in her own classroom. Sending someone to find her would not make Mrs. Leeper happy.

Friday evening, Jo Ann telephoned to ask Maggie to spend the night at her house.

Maggie said she couldn't. Jo Ann wanted to know why. Maggie said she had to help her father.

"I thought he did some kind of office work," said Jo Ann.

"He does," said Maggie, thinking fast. "I know how to use our computer." She had not lied, not exactly, but she felt guilty.

That weekend, Maggie studied every bit of cursive writing she could find: her mother's tipping-over-backward grocery list, Ms. Madden's neat handwritten notes mixed in with papers her father brought home from the office, anything. She did not try to read her father's writing. She knew it was hopeless.

Maggie spent most of her time in her room with her door closed. With Kisser's nose resting on her foot and some old work papers in front of her, she frantically practiced cursive, including the difficult capitals:

Q W F

"What are you doing, Maggie?" asked her mother through the door.

"Nothing," answered Maggie, aware that her mother felt children were entitled to privacy and would not open the door. Letting her parents know she had changed her mind would make Maggie feel ashamed, like admitting she had been wrong.

Maggie worked hard, and by Sunday evening she agreed with what Mrs. Leeper had been saying all along: Many cursive letters are shaped like printed letters. She knew she could read cursive as long as it was neat. She practiced her signature with her letters leaning into the wind:

Maggie Schultz Maggie Schultz

When she had finished, Maggie's face was flushed, her hair more tousled than usual, but she could write cursive. Maybe it wasn't perfect, but anyone past the second grade could read it. She went to her father, who was working at the computer. "Daddy, listen to me," she said, and her voice was stern.

Mr. Schultz turned from the keyboard. "Okay, Maggie, what's up?"

"In writing, neatness counts," Maggie informed him.

"I expect it does," he agreed.

"Then you should learn to close your loops and put the right number of peaks on your *u*'s and write neatly," said Maggie.

"Funny, Ms. Madden says the same thing," said Mr. Schultz. "I'll try. Cross my heart."

Maggie was not sure she believed him. Next, Maggie went to her mother and announced, "You should make your writing lean the other way like it's supposed to and stop putting silly circles over your *i*'s."

Mrs. Schultz smiled and pushed Maggie's hair back from her flushed face. "I don't know about that, Angelface," she said. "Everyone says my handwriting is distinguished."

Maggie was tired and cross. "Well, it's wrong," she said, and she sighed so hard that Kisser looked anxious. Grown-ups were so hard to reform—maybe impossible.

Chapter 8

On Monday, Maggie looked at the words Mrs. Leeper had written on the chalkboard and discovered she was reading them because *she couldn't help it.* Mrs. Leeper had written:

This is going to be a happy week. We are going on a field trip.

Maggie was eager to carry the next message. She did not have to wait long for Mrs. Leeper to write a note for the principal. As soon as she closed the door—quietly, no slamming—Maggie slipped out the note that was written on the back of an old arithmetic paper and read the neatly formed words:

Maggie is now reading cursive. I saw her reading what I had written on the chalkboard. If she can read it, she can write it. She just won't admit it.

Maggie was shocked. Maggie was angry.

Mrs. Leeper had guessed she would peek. Maybe she had guessed all along, and now that Maggie could read cursive, she was saying mean things about her. But worst of all, Mrs. Leeper was waiting for an answer.

Maggie wanted to crumple the note, but if she did that, Mrs. Leeper would want to know why Mr. Galloway had not sent a reply. She returned the note to its tattered envelope, dragged her feet into the principal's office, and thrust it at him. She stood staring at the floor while he read it.

"Um-hm," he murmured, and Maggie heard his pen move across paper. "There you go, Maggie," he said as he handed the remains of the envelope back to her. "Thank you."

"You're welcome," said Maggie, and she got out of his office as fast as she could without running.

I won't peek, I won't peek, she told herself, but of course, she finally had to peek. What normal third grader wouldn't want to know what the principal had to say in time of crisis? This note said:

Hooray! I can tell by the way she behaves that you are right. Good teaching, Laura! I knew you could do it.

Congratulations, Maggie!

Figuring out the long word before her name took a while, and then—well! First of all, Maggie was astonished that Mr. Galloway would call a teacher by her first name. Then Maggie was indignant. Mrs. Leeper hadn't done a thing. Maggie had done all the work, and now her teacher was getting all the credit.

Maggie dreaded returning to her classroom. She plodded along, trying to figure out how she could avoid it. She couldn't, not even if she took time to go to the bathroom. Sooner or later she had to face her teacher.

With red cheeks, she handed her teacher the remains of the envelope and was about to hurry to her seat when Mrs. Leeper caught her hand, pulled Maggie to her, gave her a big hug, and said, "I don't think we need a message monitor anymore. Anyway, the envelope is worn out." She tossed it, along with the note, into the wastebasket and said, "This is a happy day, Maggie."

Maggie was both pleased and confused. She had expected Mrs. Leeper to say something about cursive, but the teacher had not. She had not even said, "It's about time," or "I knew you could do it." She just smiled at Maggie, who finally felt she could smile back.

"You know something, Mrs. Leeper?" Maggie said shyly. "Your cursive is neater than any other teacher's cursive."

Mrs. Leeper laughed. "It has to be. I'm the one who teaches it."

Maggie walked slowly to her seat. She could now make her letters flow together, and she had made her teacher happy, but maybe when she grew up and did not have to please grown-ups all the time, she might decide not to write cursive. She could print anytime she wanted. She had plenty of time to think it over.

"Muggie Maggie," said Kirby. "Teacher's pet."

Maggie decided against pushing the table into his stomach.

Instead, she sat down and wrote a note in cursive, which she shoved across the table:

You stop pushing the table into my stomick.
Sinseerly,
Maggie

Beverly Cleary is one of America's most popular authors. Born in McMinnville, Oregon, she lived on a farm in Yamhill until she was six and then moved to Portland. After college, as the children's librarian in Yakima, Washington, she was challenged to find stories for non-readers. She wrote her first book, HENRY HUGGINS, in response to a boy's question, "Where are the books about kids like us?"

Mrs. Cleary's books have earned her many prestigious awards, including the American Library Association's Laura Ingalls Wilder Award, presented in recognition of her lasting contribution to children's literature. Her DEAR MR. HENSHAW was awarded the 1984 John Newbery Medal, and both RAMONA QUIMBY, AGE 8 and RAMONA AND HER FATHER have been named Newbery Honor Books. In addition, her books have won more than thirty-five statewide awards based on the votes of her young readers. Her characters, including Henry Huggins, Ellen Tebbits, Otis Spofford, and Beezus and Ramona Quimby, as well as Ribsy, Socks, and Ralph S. Mouse, have delighted children for generations. Mrs. Cleary lives in coastal California.

Visit Beverly Cleary on the World Wide Web at www.beverlycleary.com.

1

Ramona's Great Day

"I am *not* a pest," Ramona Quimby told her big sister Beezus.

"Then stop acting like a pest," said Beezus, whose real name was Beatrice. She was standing by the front window waiting for her friend Mary Jane to walk to school with her.

"I'm not acting like a pest. I'm singing and skipping," said Ramona, who had only recently learned to skip with both feet. Ramona did not think she was a pest. No matter what others said, she never thought she was a pest. The people who called her a pest were always bigger and so they could be unfair.

Ramona went on with her singing and skipping. "This is a great day, a great day, a great day!" she sang, and to Ramona, who was feeling grown up in a dress instead of play clothes, this was a great day, the greatest day of her whole life. No longer would she have to sit on her tricycle watching Beezus and Henry Huggins and the rest of the boys and girls in the neighborhood go off to school. Today she was going to school, too. Today she was going to learn to read and write and do all the things that would help her catch up with Beezus.

"Come *on*, Mama!" urged Ramona, pausing in her singing and skipping. "We don't want to be late for school."

"Don't pester, Ramona," said Mrs. Quimby. "I'll get you there in plenty of time."

"I'm *not* pestering," protested Ramona, who never meant to pester. She was not a slowpoke grown-up. She was a girl who could not wait. Life was so interesting she had to find out what happened next.

Then Mary Jane arrived. "Mrs. Quimby, would it be all right if Beezus and I take Ramona to kindergarten?" she asked.

"No!" said Ramona instantly. Mary Jane was one of those girls who always wanted to pretend she was a mother and who always wanted Ramona to be the baby. Nobody was going to catch Ramona being a baby on her first day of school.

"Why not?" Mrs. Quimby asked Ramona. "You could walk to school with Beezus and Mary Jane just like a big girl."

"No, I couldn't." Ramona was not fooled for an instant. Mary Jane would talk in that silly voice she used when she was being a mother and take her by the hand and help her across the street, and everyone would think she really was a baby.

"Please, Ramona," coaxed Beezus. "It

4

would be lots of fun to take you in and intro-
duce you to the kindergarten teacher."

"No!" said Ramona, and stamped her
foot. Beezus and Mary Jane might have fun,
but she wouldn't. Nobody but a genuine
grown-up was going to take her to school. If
she had to, she would make a great big noisy
fuss, and when Ramona made a great big
noisy fuss, she usually got her own way. Great
big noisy fusses were often necessary when a
girl was the youngest member of the family
and the youngest person on her block.

"All right, Ramona," said Mrs. Quimby.
"Don't make a great big noisy fuss. If that's
the way you feel about it, you don't have to
walk with the girls. I'll take you."

"Hurry, Mama," said Ramona happily, as
she watched Beezus and Mary Jane go out
the door. But when Ramona finally got her
mother out of the house, she was disap-
pointed to see one of her mother's friends,

Mrs. Kemp, approaching with her son Howie and his little sister Willa Jean, who was riding in a stroller. "Hurry, Mama," urged Ramona, not wanting to wait for the Kemps. Because their mothers were friends, she and Howie were expected to get along with one another.

"Hi, there!" Mrs. Kemp called out, so of course Ramona's mother had to wait.

Howie stared at Ramona. He did not like having to get along with her any more than she liked having to get along with him.

Ramona stared back. Howie was a solid-looking boy with curly blond hair. ("Such a waste on a boy," his mother often remarked.) The legs of his new jeans were turned up, and he was wearing a new shirt with long sleeves. He did not look the least bit excited about starting kindergarten. That was the trouble with Howie, Ramona felt. He never got excited. Straight-haired Willa Jean, who was interesting to Ramona because she was so sloppy, blew out a mouthful of wet zwieback crumbs and laughed at her cleverness.

"Today my baby leaves me," remarked Mrs. Quimby with a smile, as the little group proceeded down Klickitat Street toward Glenwood School.

Ramona, who enjoyed being her mother's baby, did not enjoy being called her mother's baby, especially in front of Howie.

"They grow up quickly," observed Mrs. Kemp.

Ramona could not understand why grown-ups always talked about how quickly children grew up. Ramona thought growing up was the slowest thing there was, slower even than waiting for Christmas to come. She had been waiting years just to get to kindergarten, and the last half hour was the slowest part of all.

When the group reached the intersection

nearest Glenwood School, Ramona was pleased to see that Beezus's friend Henry Huggins was the traffic boy in charge of that particular corner. After Henry had led them across the street, Ramona ran off toward the kindergarten, which was a temporary wooden building with its own playground. Mothers and children were already entering the open door. Some of the children looked fright-ened, and one girl was crying.

"We're late!" cried Ramona. "Hurry!"

Howie was not a boy to be hurried. "I don't see any tricycles," he said critically. "I don't see any dirt to dig in."

Ramona was scornful. "This isn't nursery school. Tricycles and dirt are for nursery school." Her own tricycle was hidden in the garage, because it was too babyish for her now that she was going to school.

1

The Kitten Sale

The tabby kitten hooked his white paws over the edge of the box marked, *Kittens 25¢ or Best Offer.* The girl with the stringy hair and sunburned arms picked him up and set him down in the midst of his wiggling, crawling, mewing brothers and sisters. He wanted to get out; she wanted him to stay in. The puzzling struggle had gone on all morning in the space between the mailbox and the newspaper rack near the door of the supermarket.

"Nice fresh kittens for sale," called out the girl, whose name was Debbie. She usually held the kitten in her arms, and he expected her to hold him now.

"Stupid," said her brother George, embarrassed to be selling kittens with his younger sister on a summer morning. "Whoever heard of fresh kittens?"

"Me," said Debbie, as she pushed the kitten down once more. Then she repeated at the top of her voice, "Nice fresh kittens for sale." She knew she was not stupid, and she enjoyed annoying her brother. The two had quarreled at breakfast. George said Debbie should sell the kittens, because she played with them and that made them hers. Debbie said George should sell the kittens, because she didn't know how to make change. Besides, he was the one who had

brought the mother
home when she was a kitten, so that
made her kittens his. Their father said, "Stop
bickering, you two. You can both sell them,"
and that was that.

The white-pawed kitten, unaware of the
hard feelings between brother and sister, tried

3

again. He stepped on another kitten and this time managed to lift his chin over the rim of the carton. His surprised blue eyes took in a parking lot full of shoppers pushing grocery carts among cars glittering in the summer heat. He was fascinated and frightened.

"Now Socks," said Debbie, as she unhooked his claws from the cardboard, "be a good kitten."

Socks's orange-and-white sister caught his tail and bit it. Socks rolled over on his back and swiped at her with one white paw. He no longer felt playful toward a littermate who bit his tail. Now that he was seven weeks old, he wanted to escape from all the rolling, pouncing, and nipping that went on inside the box.

Unfortunately, no shopper was willing to buy Socks his freedom. Several paused to smile at the sign, and then Socks found himself shoved to the bottom of the heap by

Debbie.

"What are you going to do with all the money when you sell the kittens?" asked an elderly woman who was lonely for her grandchildren.

"Daddy says we should save up to have the mother cat shoveled, so she won't have kittens all the time," answered Debbie.

"Spayed," corrected George. "She means he said we should have the mother spayed."

"Oh, my," said the woman and hurried into the market.

"Stupid," said George. "Anyway, Dad was joking, I think."

This time Debbie looked as if she agreed with her brother that she might be stupid. "What are we going to do?" she asked, as she plucked Socks from the edge of the carton once more. "Nobody wants them."

"Mark them down, I guess. Dad said to *give* them away if we had to." The boy borrowed a felt-tipped pen from a checker in the market and, while Socks peered over the edge of the carton, crossed out the *25¢* on his sign and wrote *20¢* above it.

"Kittens for sale." Debbie's voice sounded encouraging as she hid Socks under two of his littermates. He promptly wiggled out. On a day like this his own fur was warm enough.

"Why do you keep hiding Socks?" George tried to look as if he just happened to be standing there by the mailbox and had nothing to do with the kittens.

"Because he's the best kitten, and I want to keep him," said Debbie.

"Dad won't let you," her brother reminded her. "He says the house is getting to smell like cats."

Socks found himself plucked from the litter and cradled in the girl's arms. "Well, at least we can find a good home for him."

Debbie was admitting the truth of her brother's statement. "I don't want just anybody to take Socks."

"You don't see a line of people forming to buy kittens, do you?" asked George. To pass the time he had read the headlines of the newspapers in the rack and the label on the mailbox and was starting in on the signs posted in the windows of the market.

Socks tried to climb Debbie's T-shirt, but she held him back while she watched the faces of shoppers for signs of interest. Once a man approached, but he only wanted to drop a letter in the mailbox. A woman paused long enough to look at each kitten and then say, "No, I can't bear to think of anything as warm and furry as a kitten on such a hot day."

Children entering the market with their parents begged to be allowed to buy a kitten, just one, please, *please*, with their very own money, but no one actually bought a kitten. "I guess it just isn't kitten weather," said Debbie.

Socks struggled to free himself from the heat of the girl's sweaty arms. "Be good, Socks," said Debbie. "We're trying to find you a nice home."

"Fat chance." George had finished reading the signs in the window and was even more bored. Special prices on ground beef and soap and announcements of cake sales did not interest him.

A woman with her hair on rollers, wearing a muumuu and rubber-thong sandals, herded three children and a tired-looking mongrel across the parking lot. The tallest, a girl barely old enough to read, shrieked, "Mommy, look! A kitten sale!"